Chloe the Chameleon
D0539831
Celia Warren
Illustrated by Rob Hefferan
RIGBY

Chloe the chameleon
was good at catching flies.
Chloe could see the flies
but they couldn't see her.
Then with a flick and a lick,
she got them!

One day Chloe was sitting on a big, red flower.
Chloe was red too.
Suddenly a fly landed on Chloe's nose.
A flick – a lick – but the fly was too quick!
It got away.

The fly went on to an orange flower.
Chloe went after the fly.
Soon Chloe was orange too.

Then the fly landed on Chloe's nose.

A flick – a lick – but the fly was too quick!

It got away.

The fly went on to some yellow sand.
Chloe followed the fly and
soon Chloe was yellow too.

Then the fly landed on Chloe's nose.

A flick – a lick – but the fly was too quick!

It got away.

The fly landed on a green leaf.
Chloe climbed the tree and
soon Chloe was as green as the leaf.

Then the fly landed on Chloe's nose.

A flick – a lick – but the fly was too quick!

It got away.

The fly flew up into the blue sky.
Chloe climbed up the tree and
soon Chloe was as blue as the sky.

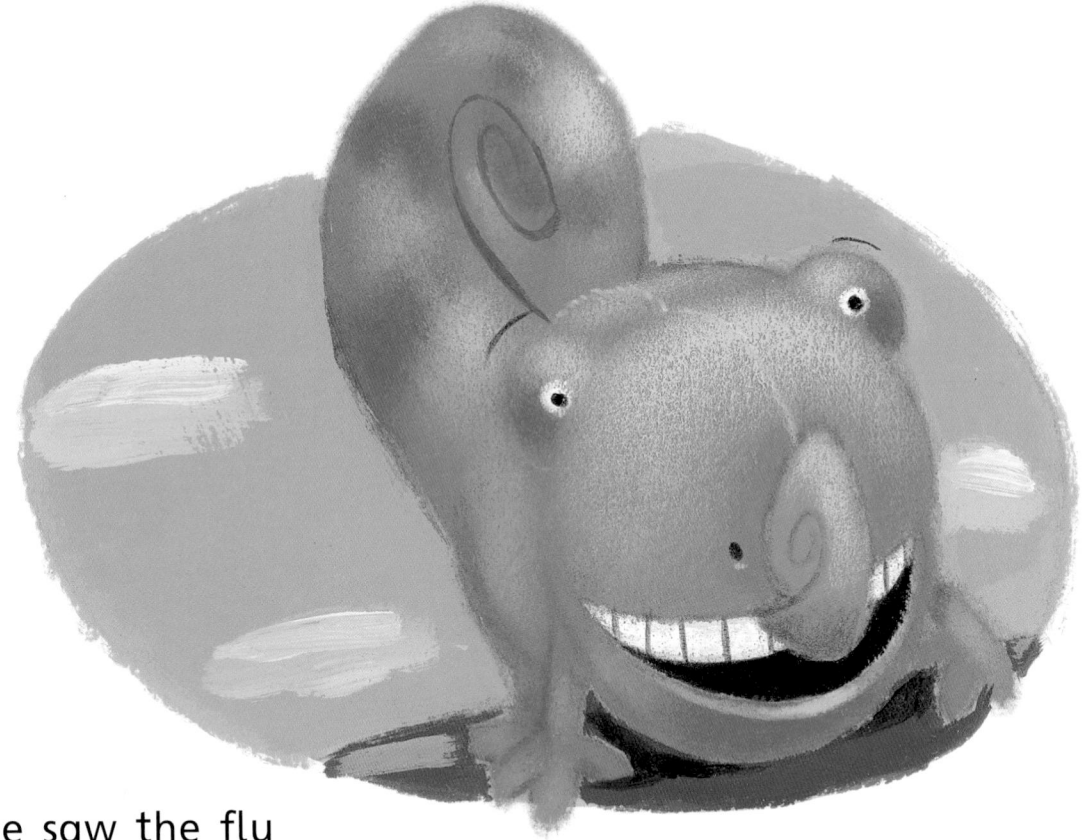

Chloe saw the fly
but the fly didn't see Chloe.
A flick – a lick – but the fly was too quick!
It got away.

The fly flew up into the sky.
Chloe climbed up the tree.
The sky got darker.
Soon the sky was indigo.
Chloe was indigo too.

Chloe saw the fly
but the fly didn't see Chloe.
A flick – a lick – but the fly was too quick!
It got away.

The sky got darker and darker.
Soon it was violet and
Chloe was violet too.
Then it began to rain.

With a flick and a lick – Chloe was quick!
This time she got the fly!

But Chloe slipped!
She fell
down,
down,
down,
through the rainbow.

Chloe sat in the sun
and waited for another fly...